POLICE on Patrol

By Annie Auerbach
Illustrated by Jesus Redondo & Ivan & Moxo

LITTLE SIMON
An imprint of Simon & Schuster Children's Publishing Division
New York   London   Toronto   Sydney   Singapore
1230 Avenue of the Americas
New York, New York 10020

Manufactured in the United States of America
First Edition
2   4   6   8   10   9   7   5   3   1
ISBN 0-689-85896-5

Early Monday morning a group of officers assembled in the Hero City police station for roll call.

"Settle down, everyone," said the police lieutenant. "I know you're anxious to hit the streets and start your shift."

The lieutenant updated the officers on things they should watch out for on their patrols. "That's it for now. Be safe."

Officer Matt Sheldon and his partner, Officer Barbara Torres, headed to their patrol car. They worked together patrolling the same beat—beat number sixteen. They made a great team.

"Shall I drive?" asked Officer Sheldon.

Officer Torres laughed. "Every day you try that. No way! Now get in and buckle up!"

Suddenly a call came through from the dispatcher. "One Adam-sixteen. Code two."
Officer Sheldon picked up the hand radio and said, "Sixteen. Go ahead."
"We have a huge traffic pileup at the intersection of First and Hill," continued the dispatcher.
"Copy," replied Officer Sheldon. "We're on our way."

Officer Torres turned on the red-and-blue flashing lights. The siren wailed as she floored the gas pedal. She expertly weaved in and out of traffic, safely and carefully.

"You're the best driver on the street," Matt said to his partner.

"I know," Barbara replied with a chuckle. "I *love* driving this police car!"

Before long the officers arrived at the scene. A truck had crashed. There were piles of stinky fish everywhere!

No one seemed to be hurt, so Officer Torres asked, "What exactly happened?"

"A dog ran right in front of my car," a woman replied. "I swerved so I wouldn't hit the poor little fella and—"

"And you plowed right into me!" a truck driver interrupted.

"Calm down. Calm down," Officer Torres told them.

Meanwhile Officer Sheldon began to direct traffic. He directed traffic with one hand and held his nose with the other!

Eventually tow trucks were called in. By lunchtime a cleanup crew had arrived to pick up the stinky fish.

Back in the patrol car Officer Torres joked, "Let's not have fish for lunch!"
"I agree!" said Officer Sheldon with a laugh.

After lunch the officers patrolled the neighborhood.

Another call came in around 1:35 P.M. "One Adam-sixteen. Code three."

"Sixteen. Go ahead," Officer Sheldon responded.

"Four fifty-nine in progress. Burglary at Hero City Bank," said the dispatcher.

"Copy. We're en route," said Officer Sheldon.

With the lights flashing and siren blaring, the patrol car sped through the streets. It was the police to the rescue!

The officers arrived just as the robber hopped in his truck. The officers took off after the truck.

The chase was on!

The truck darted in and out of traffic. Officers Torres and Sheldon were close behind. They weren't about to let the suspects escape.

But the suspects weren't about to give up either. They pulled a quick U-turn and headed right for the officers' patrol car!

Officer Torres swerved to the right just in time. Then she turned around and pursued the truck. The high-speed chase continued!

Just then Officer Sheldon radioed for backup. He reported that the suspects were driving down Sunnyslope Avenue. As soon as the other officers arrived, they set up a spike strip. It was time for some teamwork!

RIP! BOOM! BLAM!

The truck went right over the spike strip, causing its front tires to blow out. The driver tried to maintain control, but the car went swirling around and around in circles before crashing into a fire hydrant.

Then the suspects took off on foot!

W 9568

But no one can outrun a police vehicle—especially with Officer Torres behind the wheel!

She cornered the suspects in an alley, and Officer Sheldon leaped out of the car. "Police! Don't move!" he called. "Hands behind your heads!"

The two officers took the suspects into custody, read them their rights, and put them in the back of the police car.

The officers brought the suspects into the police station, booked them, and returned to their patrol car to finish out their shift.

Just then a dog ran right in front of their patrol car!

SCREECH! went the brakes as Officer Torres made a quick stop. "Good thing we were wearing our seat belts!" she said.

The police officers jumped out of their patrol car and approached the dog. "Be careful," Officer Torres reminded her partner. "You shouldn't touch a strange dog. He might attack." But the dog happily ran over to the officers.

Officer Sheldon found a dog tag on the dog's neck. "Two Gershwin Drive," he read.

"Maybe he was the cause of the accident back on First Street," Officer Torres pointed out. "Let's take him home."

Officer Torres drove to the house listed on the dog's tag. A young boy answered the door.

"You found Follie!" the boy exclaimed. "I thought he was gone forever!"

"This dog needs to be kept on a leash when you take him outside," Officer Sheldon explained.

"Okay, officer," said the boy, as the dog licked his face.

The officers headed back to their patrol car. Their shift was finally over. "Come on, let's go back to the station," said Officer Torres. "It's been quite a day!" Then she tossed the keys to Officer Sheldon. "I'll even let you drive!" she added with a smile.